Alpacas

Heather Hammonds

Contents

Alpacas

Alpacas are farm animals that grow a thick coat, called a fleece.
Their soft, warm fleece can be made into **yarn**.
The yarn is used for things like clothes and rugs.

Alpacas have a long neck, large eyes and pointed ears.
They have two large toes on each foot.

Alpacas were first kept as farm animals
in South America.
Now they live on farms all around the world.

Some alpacas grow a thick, fluffy fleece.
Other alpacas grow a longer fleece
that hangs down each side of their body.

A Helpful Farm Animal

Alpacas often live in a herd, on an alpaca farm.
Sometimes, they live with sheep and goats.
Alpacas can help keep sheep and goats safe
from other animals like foxes.
Alpacas will squeal at the animals
and chase them away!

Alpacas and sheep live together in this herd.

Most alpacas live on farms with strong fences and a shed for shelter.
The alpacas go into their shed during hot weather, or on cold, windy days.

Alpacas eat fresh grass and hay.
They drink lots of fresh water, too.

Baby Alpacas

Baby alpacas are called crias (say: *cree-yas*). Most crias are born during the day.

Other alpacas in the herd sometimes stay with the mother while her cria is born.

Little crias can sit up soon after they are born. Then they stand up on wobbly legs. They soon get a drink of milk from their mother.

Crias learn to eat grass and hay as they grow older. They drink milk from their mother for about six months.

Shearing Time

Thick, warm alpaca fleece grows very long.

Most alpacas need their fleece cut once a year.
This is called shearing.

Often, farmers have the shearing done in spring,
so their alpacas will have shorter fleece
in spring and summer.
Then the alpacas will stay cool on hot days.

These alpacas have been sheared.

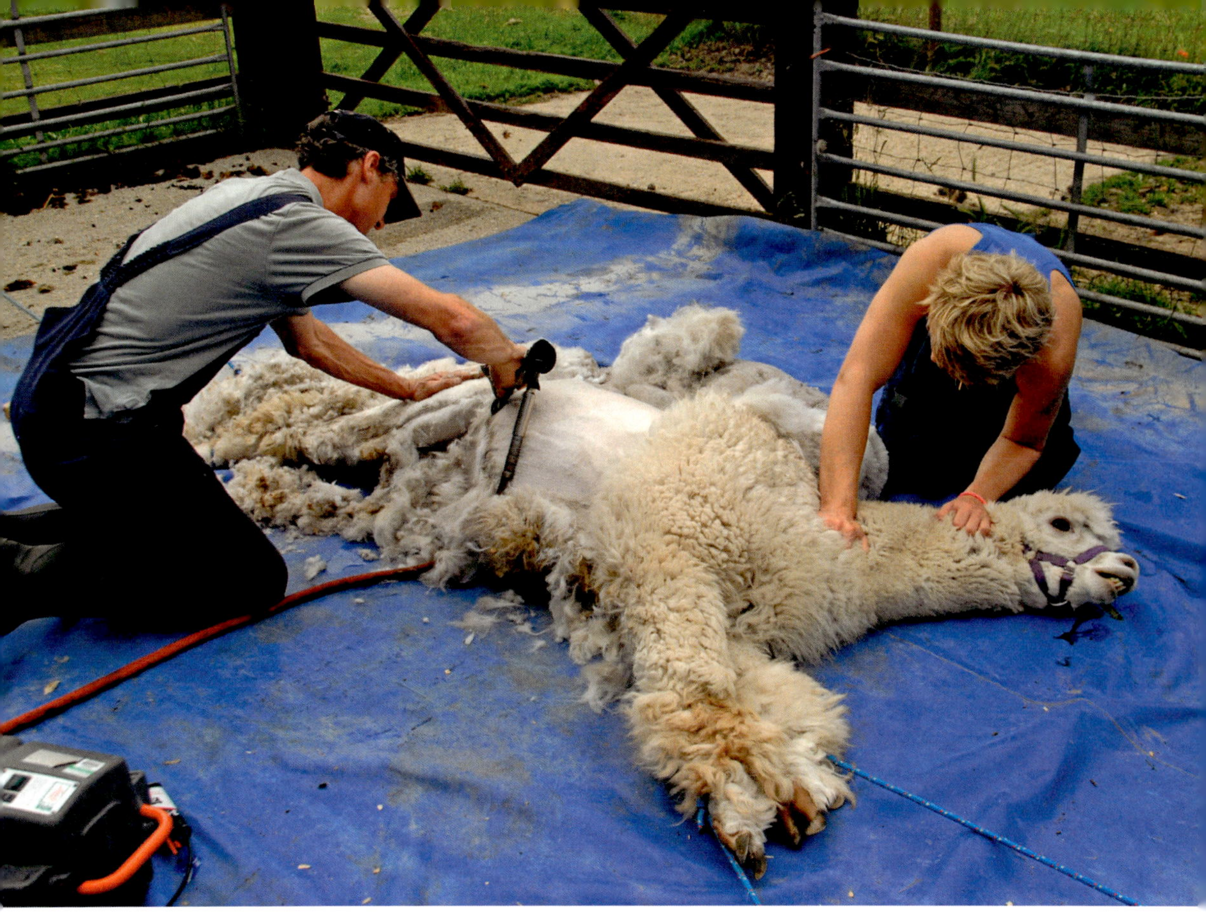

On some alpaca farms, a **shearer** comes to shear the alpacas.

The farmer and shearer lay each alpaca on its side. Then the shearer cuts its fleece. Shearing does not hurt the alpaca.

The farmer helps keep the alpaca safe and still while the shearer works.

Made from Alpaca Fleece

After shearing, alpaca fleece is sometimes sent to a **mill**.

At the mill, the fleece is cleaned and sorted.
Then, it can be made into yarn or **felt**.
It can be put inside quilts, too.

Clothing, carpets and rugs can be made
from alpaca fleece.

This woman is spinning alpaca fleece into yarn.

Some people spin their own alpaca fleece into yarn.
They make their own beautiful clothing
from the yarn.
Clothing made from alpaca fleece is warm and soft.

Alpacas on Show

Many farmers take their animals to alpaca shows. Alpacas can win lots of ribbons at shows.

Alpacas are led around a circle called a show ring. A judge looks at things like the alpaca's fleece and their body shape.

The judge picks which alpaca they think is the best in each group.

Alpacas can go through
an **obstacle course** at shows, too.

There are lots of things to see and do
at alpaca shows!

An alpaca goes through an obstacle course.

Alpacas and Llamas

Alpacas and llamas (say: *la-mas*) look a little bit like each other.

Llamas are farm animals from South America, too. They are from the same family of animals as alpacas.

Llamas are much bigger and stronger than alpacas. They have longer ears and a longer nose, too.

Many farmers keep alpacas for their beautiful fleece. Clothing made from alpaca fleece looks good, and it is nice and warm!

It is fun to keep alpacas or to visit an alpaca show.

Glossary

felt (*noun*) a kind of thick cloth that can be made from fleece

mill (*noun*) a factory with machines for making things like yarn

obstacle course (*noun*) a path with jumps, water or other things that people or animals can go through

shearer (*noun*) a person who cuts, or "shears", the fleece from alpacas

yarn (*noun*) thick thread used in knitting and spinning that can be made from fleece